Topsy and Tim
First Sleepover

By Jean and Gareth Adamson

Illustrations by Belinda Worsley

LADYBIRD BOOKS

UK | USA | Canada | Ireland | Australia
India | New Zealand | South Africa

Ladybird Books is part of the Penguin Random House group of companies
whose addresses can be found at global.penguinrandomhouse.com.

ladybird.com

First published by Ladybird Books Ltd, 2016

001

Ladybird and the Ladybird logo are registered trademarks owned by Ladybird Books Ltd
The moral right of the author and illustrator has been asserted

Printed in China

A CIP catalogue record for this book is available from the British Library

ISBN: 978–0–241–18970–2

www.topsyandtim.com

This Topsy and Tim book belongs to

_____

WITHDRAWN

Topsy and Tim were going to have a sleepover at
Tony Welch's house. They were very excited. It would
be their first night away from Mummy and Dad.

They made two big piles of clothes and toys on the floor.
Mummy and Dad gave them each an overnight case.
"You won't need to take all that," Mummy said.
"You're only going for one night," Dad added.

Topsy and Tim started all over again. They packed their washing things and toothbrushes, their pyjamas and some clean clothes.

"I wish we could take Kitty with us," said Topsy.
"And Roly Poly," said Tim.

"Why don't you take your teddies?" said Mummy.
"No," said Tim. "Tony will think we're babies if we
take our teddies to bed with us."
"Well, I'm taking mine," said Topsy.

When they were ready, Dad took them to Tony's house.
Tony and his mum were waiting for them.

"Come and see where you're going to sleep," said Tony.
They all raced upstairs.
"Bye! Be good," Dad called after them.

There was a folding bed in Tony's room,
next to Tony's bed.
"That's your bed, Tim," said Tony.
"Where's my bed?" asked Topsy.

"Here," said Tony, jumping on to a mattress on the floor.
"Lucky you!" said Tim.
They all started to bounce on Topsy's bed.
It made a good trampoline. Tony's mum
heard the noise and came upstairs.
"Tea's ready," she said.

Tony's mum gave them their favourite tea.
"It's like a party," said Topsy.
"It is a party," said Tony.

After tea, Topsy and Tim and Tony went out
to play football in the garden.

Then they took turns to ride Tony's bike. When it was Tim's turn, Topsy didn't want to get off the bike. Tim gave her a push. Topsy wobbled and fell off and the bike fell on top of her. "Ow! Ow! Ow!" cried Topsy.

Tony's mum came running to see what was wrong.
"I want my mummy," sobbed Topsy.
Tony's mum gave her a cuddle and soon she felt better.

It was nearly bedtime. Topsy got out of her muddy clothes and changed into her clean pyjamas.

Then Tony's mum called the boys in.
They were rather muddy, too.
"We've had a lovely time," said Tim.
"I can see you have," said Tony's mum.
Tony and Tim brushed their teeth and
washed their faces.

When Tony's mum came to tuck them up in bed,
Tony was lying down, cuddling his big, old teddy bear.
Tim was sitting up and he didn't look happy at all.
"Are you all right, Tim?" asked Tony's mum.

"I want to go home," said Tim.

"Oh, dear," said Tony's mum.

"I think you are feeling homesick."

Topsy got out of bed and came to cheer Tim up.
She was cuddling her teddy.
"I wish I'd brought my teddy," said Tim.

"You have," said Tony's mum. "He's in your bag."
"Mummy must have packed him after all," said Topsy.
Soon Topsy and Tim and Tony were all tucked up with
their teddies beside them.
"Sleep well," said Tony's mum. "We'll have lots more
fun tomorrow."

After Tony's mum had gone downstairs,
Tony said, "I don't feel like going to sleep."
Topsy and Tim didn't feel sleepy either. Soon they were
having a lovely game of shadow puppets in their room.

When Tony's mum looked in later that night, Tony's bedroom was in a mess but Topsy and Tim and Tony were all fast asleep. And their teddies were, too.

*Now turn the page and help
Topsy and Tim solve a puzzle.*

Topsy and Tim are packing to go home.
Look at the items in the panel opposite and
see if you can find them all in the big picture.

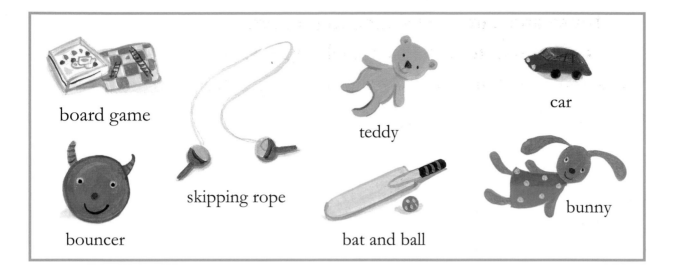

board game

teddy

car

skipping rope

bouncer

bat and ball

bunny

A Map of the Village

farm

Topsy and
Tim's house

Tony's
house

Kerr
hou

park

garage

post
office

health
centre

church

primary school

nursery school

police station

Have you read all the Topsy and Tim stories?

 **Topsy** and **Tim** — The New Baby — Jean and Gareth Adamson — seen TV
☐ 9781409300564

 **Topsy** and **Tim** — Have a Birthday Party — Jean and Gareth Adamson — seen TV
☐ 9781409300618

Topsy and **Tim** — Go on an Aeroplane — Jean and Gareth Adamson — seen TV
☐ 9781409300571

 **Topsy** and **Tim** — Play Football — Jean and Gareth Adamson — seen TV
☐ 9781409303350

Topsy and **Tim** — Go on a Train — Jean and Gareth Adamson
☐ 9781409304241

 **Topsy** and **Tim** — Learn to Swim — Jean and Gareth Adamson — seen TV
☐ 9781409300601

 **Topsy** and **Tim** — Start School — Jean and Gareth Adamson — seen TV
☐ 9781409300830

 **Topsy** and **Tim** — Go Camping — Jean and Gareth Adamson — seen TV
☐ 9781409303336

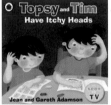 **Topsy** and **Tim** — Go to Hospital — Jean and Gareth Adamson — seen TV
☐ 9781409304234

Topsy and **Tim** — Go to the Zoo — Jean and Gareth Adamson — seen TV
☐ 9781409300847

Topsy and **Tim** — Go to the Dentist — Jean and Gareth Adamson — seen TV
☐ 9781409300588

 **Topsy** and **Tim** — At the Farm — Jean and Gareth Adamson — seen TV
☐ 9781409303367

 **Topsy** and **Tim** — Go to the Doctor — Jean and Gareth Adamson — seen TV
☐ 9781409303343

Topsy and **Tim** — Have Itchy Heads — Jean and Gareth Adamson — seen TV
☐ 9781409307204

 **Topsy** and **Tim** — Meet the Firefighters — Jean and Gareth Adamson — seen TV
☐ 9781409307211

Topsy and **Tim** — Safety First — Jean and Gareth Adamson — seen TV
☐ 9781409308829

 Topsy and **Tim** — Meet the Police — Jean and Gareth Adamson — seen TV
☐ 9781409308836

 **Topsy** and **Tim** — Sports Day — Jean and Gareth Adamson — seen TV
☐ 9781409309468

Topsy and **Tim** — Visit London — Jean and Gareth Adamson — seen TV
☐ 9781409309475

 **Topsy** and **Tim** — Meet Father Christmas — Jean and Gareth Adamson — seen TV
☐ 9781409311591

 **Topsy** and **Tim** — Help a Friend — Jean and Gareth Adamson — seen TV
☐ 9780723292593

 **Topsy** and **Tim** — Move House — Jean and Gareth Adamson — seen TV
☐ 9780723292586

 **Topsy** and **Tim** — First Sleepover — Jean and Gareth Adamson — seen TV
☑ 9780241189702

The Topsy and Tim app is now available

Available on the App Store — ANDROID APP ON Google play

The Topsy and Tim ebook range is available through all digital retailers.

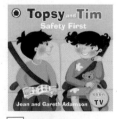